WIND OVER STONEHENGE

Pamela Dorre

 A PACEMAKER BESTELLERS™ BOOK

FEARON·PITMAN PUBLISHERS, INC.
Belmont, California

Series Director: Tom Belina
Designer: Richard Kharibian
Cover and illustrations: Rick Guidice

ISBN–0–8224–5257–1

Library of Congress Catalog Card Number: 77-75947

Printed in the United States of America.

1 9 8 7 6 5 4 3 2 1

CONTENTS

CHAPTER **1**

THE MAN IN BLACK

"So this is Stonehenge!"

Jack Austin looked at the circle of giant stones before him. The stones were almost 15 feet high. Each stone weighed many tons. It was hard to see them in the dark. The sun was not yet up.

"What a job it must have been to build this," Jack said.

The girl standing next to him nodded. "And without the tools we have today."

"Yes," Jack answered. "They didn't have any power tools 3,500 years ago. Just stone tools. Think of the work cutting the stones."

"And then moving them here," the girl said. "Professor Reed says that some of the stones came from Wales."

"That's more than 300 miles from here," Jack said. "I wonder how they moved these giant stones all that way."

"No one knows for sure," the girl said. "No one is even sure who really built Stonehenge."

Her name was Robin Steward. She and Jack had come to England with Professor Otis Reed. Professor Reed had been studying Stonehenge for a long time. He came to England every summer to try to find answers to his questions. Who built Stonehenge? Why was it built? What was it used for? But after years of study, he still did not know many of the answers.

This year Professor Reed had some new questions. And he needed help to get the answers. Which was why Jack Austin and Robin Steward were there. The Professor wanted to do some digging. Jack would help with that. And they would need pictures of anything they found. That would be Robin's job. She was good with a camera.

It was very early in the morning. Professor Reed wanted to be there when the sun came up. He walked over to Jack and Robin. "Get your camera ready, Robin. The sun will come up right over there," he said, pointing to two of the giant stones. "Right between those two stones. They are in line with the Heel Stone, over there, outside the circle."

Robin could just see the Heel Stone. It looked like a great black finger of rock. Now the sun was beginning to come up. Robin began taking pictures.

She took four or five. Then Professor Reed said, "That's enough looking that way, Robin. Now take some looking away from Stonehenge."

"The other way?" Robin asked. "But . . ."

Professor Reed smiled. "Yes," he said. "I know it sounds strange. But this is important. When the sun comes up, everyone has always looked at it toward the Heel Stone. No one has ever thought of looking the other way."

"Why should they?" Jack asked. "Why look *away* from Stonehenge?"

"Because there is more to it than just Stonehenge," Professor Reed said. "I don't know just what. But I know that there is more to it."

Robin turned her back to the sun and looked through her camera.

By now it was light. She could begin to see the land around Stonehenge better. It was flat all around. Flat and green in the early morning light.

There were some low hills off to the north of Stonehenge. Robin took pictures of the hills.

Jack was looking at the hills through a pair of field glasses. "There is something strange about one of those hills," he said. "Here, Professor Reed, take a look." He handed the field glasses to the Professor.

"Yes . . . I see what you mean," Professor Reed said. "That hill in the middle. It looks different from the hills on either side. But I'm not sure why."

"Maybe Robin's pictures will tell us," Jack said. Robin was using a special film that made colors stand out.

"I'll do the best I can," Robin said, taking another picture.

The three were standing with their backs to Stonehenge. They didn't see the man in black moving toward them. He had been watching them all this time, hiding behind one of the stones.

He was dressed all in black, with a long flowing coat. His head was covered so only his face showed. The man's eye's flashed like fire as he moved toward the three.

In his hand he held a stone ax. The head of the ax was tied to a wood handle. It was the same kind of ax used 3,500 years ago by the people who had built Stonehenge.

As he got closer, he lifted the stone ax over his head with both hands. One more step and he would be able to smash their heads.

CHAPTER 2

A WARNING

Jack saw the ax out of the corner of his eye. "Look out!" he shouted. But it was too late. The man in black swung the ax down. It just missed the Professor's head and smashed into the ground by his feet.

Jack pushed the Professor to one side and grabbed for the man in black. But the man was too quick. He jumped back and put up one hand. "Stay where you are!" he said. "You have been warned. Now go!"

"What?" said Jack, almost too surprised to speak. "What are you talking about? Who are you?"

Jack started forward toward the man. "Wait," said the Professor, holding Jack by the arm. "Let him be. Let's find out just what's going on."

The Professor turned to the man in black. "Who are you?" he asked. "Why did you just try to kill us?"

"If I had wanted to kill you," the man said, "I would have done so. That was only a warning. Now go!"

"Who do you think you are?" Robin said. "You can't tell us what to do."

"I am Odvard," the man said in a low voice. "Odvard the Druid. Stonehenge was built by my people—the Druids. And we Druids still watch over it."

"A Druid!" Professor Reed said. "There are no more Druids. The last Druids died more than a thousand years ago."

"That's what most people think," Odvard said. "But as you can see, it is not so. I am a Druid. And it is my job to watch over Stonehenge, as Druids have always done. To watch over Stonehenge and keep people like you away from its secrets, Professor Reed."

"How do you know my name?" The Professor asked, surprised.

"We Druids know many things. We have many powers."

   "Well," said Jack, "you don't have the power to keep us away from Stonehenge. The Professor has been given the right to work here this summer. By the British Museum. We are not taking orders from any Druids."

   "We Druids know things that the British Museum does not," Odvard said. "We know the many secrets of Stonehenge. These secrets must *stay* secret! For the good of us all! I ask you once again, leave this place. Return to where you came from. Forget about Stonehenge. Forget about the digging you were planning to do."

Professor Reed said, "So, you know about the digging, too. Who are you, anyway?"

Odvard said nothing for a minute. Then he stepped forward and picked up his stone ax. The sharp head of the ax flashed in the early morning sun. His face was very close to Professor Reed's face. He looked deep into the Professor's eyes. "There are some things best left alone by science," Odvard said. "Stonehenge is one of them, Professor. I tell you one last time: leave Stonehenge alone."

Then he turned and walked off.

"I think we should call the police," Robin said. "That guy is crazy."

"Does he really think that he is a Druid?" Jack asked.

"Yes," the Professor said. "I'm sure he does."

Robin said, "But there are no more Druids! You said that the last Druids died more than a thousand years ago."

"That's what we think, Robin. In fact, we know very little about the Druids. Some say that the Druids built Stonehenge. Others say they did not. Some don't even think there ever *were* any people called Druids."

"He looked real enough to me," Jack said.

Professor Reed smiled. "You mean the long black coat? The stone ax? This isn't the first time I've seen people walking around like that."

Robin and Jack both looked surprised. "Let's go have some breakfast," Otis Reed said. "I'll tell you about it on the way."

Their car was parked on the road a short way from Stonehenge. Jack got in on the driver's side. "It's a good thing we have you to drive," the Professor said. "I have been to England many times. But I still haven't got used to driving on the 'wrong' side of the road."

"I still need a bit more practice, too," Robin said, sitting back in her seat.

"You just like letting someone else do all the work," Jack laughed.

They headed north from Stonehenge toward the small town of Avebury. Avebury was a few miles from Stonehenge.

The three had driven to Stonehenge the night before, all the way from London. They had reached Stonehenge just in time to see the sun come up and for Robin to take pictures. Now they moved on to Avebury. Avebury was where they would be staying for the summer.

They headed north across the flat, green Salisbury Plain. The sky was a deep blue. It was going to be a beautiful English summer day.

"Now tell us more about these Druids," Jack said, as they rolled along.

"Well, Jack, as I said, no one really knows that much about the Druids. We don't think there are any real ones left. But there *are* people who go around *calling* themselves Druids."

"Like that crazy guy with the ax?" said Robin.

"Yes," answered the Professor. "I have seen them before at Stonehenge. They like to hang around and tell people that they are Druids. That they come from a line of people who built Stonehenge 3,500 years ago. They say they know all the secrets of Stonehenge."

"Do they?" Jack asked.

The Professor laughed. "If they do, they're not telling anyone! No, I don't think they know any secrets. These so-called Druids are just people like you and me. They just like to dress up in funny clothes and go around talking about the 'secrets' they know."

"What do the police think about these Druids?" Robin asked.

"As long as they don't bother anyone, the police leave them alone. They have a right to believe anything they want," Professor Reed answered.

"But what about that guy's stone ax?" Jack said. "He could have killed you."

"True," said the Professor. "It's not like Druids to do things like that. They all say they believe in peace. They are against killing of any kind. It *was* rather strange about the ax. But, then, he said he didn't mean to hurt me."

"I think you should tell the police," Jack said.

"Perhaps," the Professor answered. "But we have a lot to do this summer. I don't think we have time to get mixed up with police matters. Let's just forget about it. Live and let live, as the Druids say."

CHAPTER **3**

ANOTHER STONE CIRCLE

As the car neared Avebury, Jack could see more giant stones. They were as big as those at Stonehenge, but not as well made.

"What's this?" he said to Professor Reed in a surprised voice.

"The Great Stone Circle of Avebury," the Professor answered.

"You mean there is more than one?" Jack said. "I thought Stonehenge was the only . . ."

"Yes," the Professor said. "That's what most people think. Stonehenge is very famous. Not many people know that there is another Stone Circle just a few miles away."

Jack had pulled the car over and stopped. He wanted to get a better look. "It doesn't look too much like a circle to me," he said.

The stones were set on top of a great ring-shaped mound. Some were standing straight up. Others were on their sides.

14

Robin said, "It doesn't look much like a circle to me, either."

"That's because the circle is so big," Professor Reed explained. "It's a three-mile walk around the outside of the circle. The circle is so big that the whole town of Avebury is inside it. Of course, it is a very small town, but. . . ."

"The whole town! I see what you mean," said Robin. "Some circle!"

Jack started up the car again. Once they were inside the ring-shaped mound, they could see the town of Avebury. There were just a few very old stone houses and just one street—the road into town. At the far end of the street was a larger stone building with a sign: The King's Arms Inn.

Professor Reed said, "That's where we will be staying. At the King's Arms Inn. The only place around that lets out rooms."

A woman was standing in front of the Inn. When she saw Professor Reed in the car she smiled and waved.

"That's Dr. Desmond," Professor Reed said. "Cynthia Desmond. From the British Museum. She and I worked together a few years ago at Stonehenge. We will be working together again this year. She is a fine person. I think you are both going to like working with her."

Jack parked the car next to the Inn. Cynthia Desmond walked over as the three were getting out. She was a tall woman, with light brown hair, pulled back.

"Welcome to Avebury," she said. "Good to see you again, Otis."

"Good to see you again, too," Otis Reed said. "I'd like you to meet two friends of mine. They will be helping us this summer."

They talked for a few minutes. Then they got their bags and checked into The King's Arms Inn. Cynthia showed them to their rooms. She was staying at the Inn, too.

Then they came back down for an English breakfast of fish and fried eggs.

After eating, the four took a walk to look at the Stone Circle. From the top of the mound, they could see most of the great circle. Some of the stones were missing. But it was still quite a sight. A great grass-covered mound with giant stones every 30 feet or so.

Robin was busy taking pictures with her camera. "I thought we would be able to see Stonehenge from the top of the mound," she

said. "But I guess we are not really that close after all."

Professor Reed pointed. "Those hills over there are in the way," he said. "If the hills were not there, you could see Stonehenge."

Off to the south, between two of the giant stones, they could see the hills. "There," Robin said, taking a picture of the hills. "That's the last picture on this roll of film."

The next few days were busy ones. Professor Reed and Dr. Desmond worked from early morning until dark, studying the giant stones. Part of the time they spent at Avebury. Part of the time they spent at Stonehenge. They wanted to find out as much as possible about the two stone circles.

Professor Reed hoped that Robin's pictures might tell them something. Toward the end of the week, the pictures were ready. Jack and Robin drove over to Salisbury to pick them up. Robin looked at the pictures on the way back to Avebury.

"How did they turn out?" Jack asked.

"Fine, just fine," Robin answered. "I got some good pictures of the sun coming up over the Heel Stone. And the ones showing those hills north of Stonehenge turned out OK, too. You were right about that hill in the middle."

"The one that looks different from the others," Jack said.

"Yes," said Robin. "It looks *a lot* different in this picture. That special film I used really makes it stand out."

When they got back to Avebury, they showed the pictures to Professor Reed at the Inn.

"I see what you mean," the Professor said to Robin and Jack. "That hill *is* different. Not as green as the hills on either side. And not as rounded. I think we should try to find out more about that hill."

Jack said, "Look! There's something else in the picture."

On the right side of the picture was one of the giant stones.

"See that?" Jack said, pointing to the stone in the picture. "Someone was hiding behind that stone when you took the picture, Robin. You can see part of his face. He was watching us. But he didn't want us to spot him."

Robin took a close look at the picture. "You're right," she said. "And we have seen that man before. It's Odvard. Odvard the Druid!"

Professor Reed said, "I don't see any face. It's just a spot on the picture. Anyway, how could Odvard know we were here? We left him at Stonehenge."

"Maybe," said Jack. "Maybe it is just a spot. But maybe not. Remember that Odvard knew a lot of things. He knew your name. And he knew you were planning to dig. Maybe he also knew we were coming to Avebury after we left Stonehenge. He seemed to know all about your work."

Professor Reed said, "True. But I'm sure there is some easy way to explain that."

"I want to take a look at that stone in the picture," said Robin. "Anyone want to come with?"

"I'll come with," said Jack.

"I'll join you later," the Professor said.

Jack and Robin left the Inn. They climbed the mound and walked over to the stone in the picture.

"Is this the stone?" Jack said.

"I think so," Robin answered. "Yes, it's the same one."

The stone was about 15 feet high. It was a blue-gray color. It looked like a giant tooth, pointed at one end.

"Let's see if we can find anything," Jack said. "Some sign that Odvard really was here, hiding behind this stone."

Robin walked around the stone. Suddenly she cried out, "Jack! Look! Someone *was* here! He left something for us to find!"

Jack ran over to where Robin was standing. She pointed at the stone. "Look at that!" she said.

Jack's heart jumped a beat. On the stone was a simple drawing. Two men and two women. A red X had been crossed through each one.

In blood.

"I think that's supposed to be us," Robin said.

"Us dead," said Jack.

CHAPTER **4**

THE HILL

"It's probably just some children's trick," Professor Reed said, looking at the blood on the stone.

"A trick?" said Robin. "But the drawing is in blood. What kind of a trick is that?"

"Looks like chicken blood to me," said the Professor. "Really, there is nothing to worry about. Come on. Let's get to work. We have a lot to do. Jack, start getting our tools ready. I want to take a look at that strange hill tomorrow morning."

They went over to the hill early the next morning. From the bottom, it didn't look different from the other hills.

"Let's see what it looks like from the top," Cynthia Desmond said.

From the top of the hill, they could see all around. "Look," Jack said. "There's Stonehenge."

"And there's Avebury," said Robin. "This hill is right in the middle between them."

"Yes," Dr. Desmond said. "You could draw a straight line between them."

Professor Reed's eyes lighted up. "Yes!" he said. "You *could* draw a line between them. And maybe someone did! Jack, start digging. I have an idea."

"Where?" asked Jack. "Where do you want me to dig?"

"It doesn't matter," the Professor answered. "Just dig. I'll tell you when to stop."

Jack started digging into the grass-covered hill. He worked for more than an hour.

The hole was getting deep. "This is hard work," said Jack, wiping his face. "What are we looking for? So far all I've found is dirt."

The pile of dirt next to the hole was growing.

"Dirt is all I think we are going to find," Professor Reed said. "But keep digging a bit more, just to make sure."

Jack kept on digging.

At last, Professor Reed told him he could stop digging. "Just as I thought," the Professor said, lighting his pipe. "This is not a natural hill. Someone made this hill."

"How can you tell?" Jack Austin asked, climbing out of the hole.

"Because it's all dirt," the Professor explained. "If it were a natural hill, you would have hit rock by this time. And that's why it looked different in Robin's pictures."

"Why would anyone do all that work?" Jack asked.

"I'm not sure," Professor Reed answered. "But I think it has something to do with Stonehenge and Avebury. This hill is right in the middle between them, in a straight line."

Dr. Desmond said, "I wonder if something might be buried under this hill. That might be the reason it was made. To cover something up."

"There is only one way to find out," the Professor said.

Jack sat by the hole he had dug, rubbing his arms. "I hope you don't think I'm going to dig up this whole hill by myself," he said.

"Don't worry," Professor Reed said. "We will get some men to help you from Salisbury."

Dr. Desmond said, "And some of the people I work with at the British Museum will also help."

Digging started a week later. Professor Reed had been right. The hill was not a natural one. It was a giant pile of dirt.

He watched as Jack and the other men cut into the hill. Dr. Desmond was with him.

"I wonder about the people who made this hill," the Professor said. "Why did they want it to look like a natural hill?"

"Maybe they wanted everyone to think it *was* a natural hill," Dr. Desmond answered. So no one would start digging into it, looking for things that might be buried there. Maybe they wanted to hide something so that no one would ever find it."

"Yes, that could be it," Professor Reed answered. "But what? And why?"

Another week went by. Now most of the dirt from the hill had been dug away. They were close to the bottom. But they still had found nothing.

"Maybe there isn't anything buried under the hill," Robin said to the Professor.

"That could be," he answered. "But then why on earth would . . ."

Just then, Jack called out. "I think I may have found something!" he shouted. Everyone ran over to where he was digging.

"What is it?" asked Dr. Desmond.

"A stone," Jack said. "A very large stone."

Everyone started clearing the dirt away. In a few hours, they could see most of the stone. It was a giant blue stone, like the ones used to build Stonehenge. But bigger. Much bigger.

Robin took a picture with her camera. "Is this the reason the hill was built?" she asked. "To hide this giant stone?"

"It looks that way," Professor Reed answered.

"Why build a whole hill just to hide a stone?" Jack asked.

"A good question," Dr. Desmond said. "It does seem like a lot of work. There must be something very special about this stone.

They took a close look at the stone. It looked like a giant stone log lying on its side. It was about 25 feet long and seven feet wide.

"Look here," Professor Reed said. He pointed to a spot on the ground near one end of the stone. "You see that light circle in the dirt? A filled-in hole. At one time, this stone stood straight up in this hole."

"Did it fall over?" asked Jack.

"No," the Professor said. "I don't think so. It looks more like the stone was pushed over. Pushed over and then covered with this hill."

Jack said, "What do you think is so special about this stone, Professor?"

"It's too soon to say yet," Professor Reed answered. "We will know more when we stand the stone up in its hole again. Then we will take some sightings from Avebury and from Stonehenge. The sightings may give us answers to some of our questions."

Later, at lunch, they talked about the giant stone they had found.

"How do you plan to stand it up again?" Jack Austin asked. "It must weigh hundreds of tons. Will we use the truck?"

They had been using a heavy truck to carry away dirt from the hill. "No," Professor Reed said. "The truck doesn't have enough power. We will have to use jacks and ropes."

Jack turned his head and looked at the truck. It was parked on the side of the hill across from the stone. "Too bad we can't use the truck. Jacks and ropes sound like hard work. Hard on my back."

"I thought you *liked* hard work," laughed Robin.

As they sat talking, they did not see that the truck had begun to move. The brake was not on. The truck was starting to roll down the hill. Very slowly at first. Then faster and faster.

The truck's engine was off, so they did not hear it coming. Now the truck was rolling down the hill at high speed. Right at them. Still no one saw or heard it. It was almost on top of them before they saw it.

"Look out!" Robin screamed.

CHAPTER **5**

THE SKELETON UNDER THE STONE

They jumped out of the way just in time. The truck flashed past them and smashed into a tree with a loud bang.

"That was close!" Robin said, dusting herself off. "Too close."

Jack walked over to the truck and looked inside. "Someone forgot to set the parking brake. That's why the truck rolled down the hill."

The truck driver told them he was sure he had set the brake. He was very clear about it. He would never forget an important thing like that.

Later, the four talked about their close call. Robin said, "Maybe the driver was lying. Maybe he did forget to set the parking brake."

Dr. Desmond said, "I don't think so, Robin. He didn't sound like he was lying."

"Then how did it happen?" Jack said.

Professor Reed was cleaning his glasses. "It just happened," he said. "It was an accident."

"This was no accident, Professor," Jack said. "Someone must have taken off the brake. He wanted to make it look like an accident."

"You mean . . .?" Dr. Desmond said.

"Yes," said Jack. "Someone tried to kill us. And I think he may try again."

Standing the giant stone back up in its hole was a big job. They would use jacks to lift the stone a little at a time. Slowly, one end of the stone would be lifted. When it was almost back up, they would slide the stone into the hole with ropes.

It took several days to lift the stone just a little. But, at last, they could see space between the stone and the ground. Professor Reed was pleased with the work. "I think it's time to pack dirt under the stone so that we can move the jacks," he said.

"OK, Professor," Jack Austin answered.

"Be very careful," the Professor said. "If the stone slips off the jacks, you could be killed."

Jack took a close look at the space under the stone. "Don't worry," he said. "I'll be careful . . . Hey! What's this?! There's something under the stone! Look!"

"My word!" the Professor said. "A skeleton!"

Everyone came running.

"So that's the secret of the hill," Jack said. "They buried someone under the stone. I wonder who he was."

Professor Reed said, "I'm not sure the skeleton was really buried. You see the way all the bones are smashed? It looks more like the man was killed when the stone fell on him."

"An accident?" asked Jack.

"Perhaps," said the Professor. "Perhaps . . . We will know more once we have moved the skeleton out from under there."

"Move it?" said Jack. "Why?"

"We have to move it before we can stand the stone back up. I'll need the help of all of you. We will have to be very careful. The stone could slip off the jacks while we work."

They started moving the skeleton the next day. Professor Reed and Jack had to work lying down, in the space under the stone. There was not much room to move. And they had to be careful not to touch the stone above their heads.

"Here is something interesting," Professor Reed said. On one side of the skeleton was a small flat circle of stone. "Robin, get a shot of this before I move it."

Robin started forward. Suddenly she tripped and fell against the giant blue stone. "Get out from under there!" she screamed. "It's going to fall off the jacks!"

The stone began to slip. For a second it looked like it was going to fall. But it held. Jack and the Professor inched their way clear.

"Another close one," said Jack. He looked at his hands. They were shaking.

"I'm sorry," Robin said. "I think someone tripped me." She looked around, trying to guess who it was. Maybe it was one of the men who had been helping with the digging. One, a man named Edward Celtson, had a thick black beard. Celtson had been standing next to Robin when she tripped. Or so she thought. But now he was standing next to Dr. Desmond.

Robin was about to say something to Celtson. Then she decided not to. This time it was probably just an accident, she thought. She decided to try to be more careful.

They made sure that the jacks were in place before getting back to work. But everyone was glad when all the bones had been moved. They took them back to the Inn to study them.

Professor Reed and Dr. Desmond spent the next few days studying the skeleton. From the shape of the skull, they could tell that it was a man's skeleton. But it was not like other skeletons they had studied. The skull was more rounded on top.

The Professor said, "I have never seen a skull quite like it."

"Yes," Dr. Desmond answered. "It doesn't look at all like other skulls of Stonehenge Age people."

"Do you think he came from some other land?" Professor Reed asked.

Cynthia Desmond held the skull in her hands and gave it a close look. "Yes, probably," she said. "I have seen skulls from Egypt that looked a little like this one."

She picked up the flat stone circle they had found with the skeleton. "What do you make of this, Otis?" she asked.

The stone was about the size of a small plate. It was made of smooth green stone. One side of the stone was covered with marks. Lines, dots, and circles had been cut into the smooth face of the stone.

Otis Reed took the stone from Dr. Desmond. "I don't know what this stone means," he said. "I don't think it's writing."

"No," Cynthia Desmond said. "But those marks must mean something."

"Quite so, Cynthia," the Professor said. "I'm sure this stone has an important meaning. The man must have been using it for something. He had it with him when the stone fell on him."

Once the skeleton had been moved, Jack and the others got back to work. Each day they jacked the stone up a bit more. Soon it would be high enough. Then they would slide it into the hole.

At last they were ready. Professor Reed walked over to where Jack was standing. "All set?" he asked.

"Yes. Everything is ready," Jack said.

"Good," Professor Reed said. "Then let's begin."

The men grabbed the ropes and began to pull. The stone began to move. It began sliding down the pile of dirt that held it up.

"Keep pulling," Professor Reed said. "Keep it straight."

A few seconds later the stone was in the hole, standing straight up.

They had done it.

"Just think," Professor Reed said. "After 3,500 years, the stone is standing again."

A cold wind began to blow. The sky began to turn dark.

"Just in time, too," Robin said. "I think it's going to rain."

A flash of lightning lit up the sky.

CHAPTER **6**

WIND AND WEATHER

It rained all week. Saturday morning, rain was still coming down. The air had turned very cold.

Cynthia Desmond looked out the window of The King's Arms Inn. "It seems more like winter than summer," she said. "The rain is so cold."

"I heard it rains a lot in England," Robin said. "And it's true."

"Yes, we do get a lot of rain," Dr. Desmond said. "But it doesn't often rain this long or this hard."

The rain stopped as suddenly as it had begun. The next morning was bright and clear. Summer had returned. In fact, for an English summer, it was a very warm day.

Professor Reed and Dr. Desmond were taking sightings. They wanted to see what lined up with the Key Stone. This was their name for the stone they had put back up. Professor Reed felt this stone was the key to the secrets of Stonehenge and Avebury.

They found that the Key Stone lined up with the Heel Stone at Stonehenge. The Key Stone lined up with a stone at Avebury, too. It was the same stone someone had painted with blood. Professor Reed called it the Blood Stone, although the others didn't like the name.

"All three stones line up in a straight line," the Professor said to Cynthia Desmond. "You know what this means, don't you?"

"Yes," she answered. "It's hard to believe."

"But it's true," Professor Reed said. "Stonehenge and Avebury are both parts of one giant thing. Two giant stone circles in line with the Key Stone."

"But we still don't know why," Dr. Desmond said. "We still don't know what the stones were used for."

It was almost noon. The sun was burning hot. Jack came over, wiping his face. "Boy, it's hot!" he said. "Feels more like Africa than England."

"Yes," Cynthia Desmond answered. "It's really too hot to do much work. Shall we go back to the Inn?"

"Good idea," said Jack. "I could use a cool drink."

"I've never known it to be so warm," Cynthia Desmond said. "I can't wait for the sun to set. Things should cool down after dark."

But it was almost as warm that night as it had been during the day. And the next day was worse. The radio said a new heat record had been set. The ground was almost too hot to walk on. Birds fell from the trees and died of the heat. Farm animals were going wild.

"Europe is having quite a heat wave," Jack said. He sat at the Inn drinking ice water, trying to stay cool.

Robin said, "Europe is not having a heat wave. Just England. That's what the radio said."

"Strange," Dr. Desmond said. "Very strange. . . ."

The next morning it was worse than ever. The air was like fire. All the grass had turned brown. Trees had lost most of their leaves.

Then the wind began to blow. "Maybe this will cool things off," said Jack.

"Let's hope so," said Robin.

But it was not a cool wind. The air stayed as hot as ever. The wind picked up the dry dust and blew it all around. They closed the doors and windows of the Inn, but the dust still blew in.

The wind became stronger. It blew branches off the trees. Then whole trees started to blow down. A big tree next to the Inn came crashing down. One of the branches smashed against a window. Glass flew everywhere.

"Look out!" Jack shouted. He threw himself to the floor. Professor Reed wasn't quick enough. A piece of glass cut him in the face. He cried out and fell to the floor.

Dr. Desmond went over to him. "Get me some clean cloth," she said to Robin. "It's a bad cut."

Robin grabbed a cloth from the table and went over to help. There was blood all over the Professor's face.

The whole Inn was shaking because of the wind. Pieces of the roof began flying off. They smashed into the ground, breaking into bits.

"Professor Reed needs a doctor. I'm going to drive to Salisbury for help," said Jack.

He tried to open the door. But the wind held it closed. He pushed against it with all his might. Finally, it opened with a bang. The wind blew dust, dirt, and branches into the Inn. Jack put his arms over his head and started to run for the car.

He did not get far. The wind blew the sign off the front of the Inn. The sign came smashing down and knocked Jack to the ground. He lay on the ground without moving.

Robin jumped up and ran out the door. "Jack!" she cried. "Jack! Are you all right?" He wasn't moving.

"Jack!" she shouted. "Can you hear me?"

Pieces of the roof were falling all around. One piece smashed into the ground next to Jack's head. "I've got to move you," Robin said. She put her arms around him and pulled him back inside.

A few seconds later, Jack opened his eyes. "My arm," he said, his voice filled with pain. "My arm is broken . . . ."

Robin took the car key. "I'm going for help. We need a doctor."

She ran to the car. The air was filled with flying things. She jumped in the driver's seat and started the engine.

She wasn't used to driving on English roads— driving on the 'wrong' side of the road. But she had no time to worry about that. She headed toward Salisbury.

The wind blew the car from side to side. Robin held on to the steering wheel and kept going. But the wind was too strong. Just where the road went past the Key Stone, the wind blew the car off the road.

Robin hit the brakes. But it was no use. The wind picked up the car and turned it over like a toy.

For a minute, Robin didn't know where she was. Everything was spinning in front of her eyes. She shook her head and started to climb out of the car.

Off to her right, she could see the Key Stone. It was almost lost in the blowing dust and dirt. But there was something else there, too. Walking toward her through the dust was a man. A man dressed all in black.

"You were warned!" he cried over the wind. "I told you not to come here! See what you have done!" The man threw up his arms. "See the power of Stonehenge!"

It was Odvard.

CHAPTER **7**

THE POWER OF STONEHENGE

Robin opened her eyes. She was in her bed at the Inn. Cynthia Desmond was standing at the foot of the bed.

"Dr. Desmond!" Robin said, in a surprised voice. "How . . . How did I get here? The last thing I remember, Odvard was coming at me. Then everything went black . . . ."

"I found you by the car," Cynthia Desmond said. "When you didn't come back after an hour, I got worried. I took the car from the Inn and went to look for you. You must have passed out. You have quite a bump on your head."

"But what about Odvard?" Robin asked.

"You were all alone when I found you."

"Are you sure?" Robin said. "He was . . ." She stopped and listened. All was quiet. The wild wind had stopped.

Dr. Desmond guessed what Robin was thinking. "Yes," she said. "The wind has stopped. It died down just before I went to look for you."

Robin said, "What about the Professor? And Jack? Are they all right?"

"Mr. Davis, from the Inn, is looking after them," Dr. Desmond said. "Now just try to get some rest. You'll feel better in the morning."

The next morning, they all drove into Salisbury. They used the car from the Inn. Their own car would need fixing.

A doctor set Jack's arm. He looked at the bump on Robin's head. He also put a new bandage on Professor Reed's face.

On the way back, Robin told them again about Odvard. "I thought he was going to kill me," she said. "He was coming right at me, screaming about the power of Stonehenge."

"The power of Stonehenge," said Jack. "You didn't tell us about that part."

"I guess I forgot," Robin said. "Well, there he was, dressed all in black, with the wind blowing all around him. He started walking toward me. He was very angry and was screaming something about the power of Stonehenge."

"What did he mean by that?" Jack asked.

"I don't know," Robin answered. "But that's what he said. He said he had warned us not to come here. He seemed to think we had caused the wind to start blowing like that."

"Caused that storm?" Professor Reed said. "How could we?"

"Well, that's what he said, Professor. He waved his arms around and said, 'See what you have done.' I really think he believed that we caused the wind to blow."

"Does he think we caused the heat wave and the rain, too?" Professor Reed said.

"I don't know," Robin answered. "But, yes, I think he does. I got that feeling."

Back at the Inn that night, Professor Reed and Dr. Desmond were studying the green stone. Robin sat across the room, reading.

Jack came over to the table where they were working. "I've been thinking," Jack said.

"About what, Jack?" Professor Reed said.

"About Odvard. About what he said to Robin. What if he is right?"

Professor Reed smiled. "That's just silly. There is no way we could have caused a wind storm or a heat wave. No one can do that."

Robin had been listening to Jack's words. "Is it, Professor?" she said. "Is it really so silly? Odvard has been trying to get us to leave ever since we came here. Maybe he knows something we don't."

"Like what?" said Professor Reed. "I have studied Stonehenge for years. As a man of science, I think I know more about it than some so-called Druid." He turned and went back to studying the green stone.

"But science doesn't know everything, Otis," Cynthia Desmond said. "I think we should

listen to Jack and Robin. Go on, Jack. What did you have in mind?"

"Maybe there is some kind of . . ." He was trying to find the right word. ". . . Some kind of *power* in the stone circles. And maybe we did something to set that power working."

"How could we do that?" Cynthia Desmond said in a surprised voice.

"By setting the Key Stone back up," Jack Austin said.

"And what was that supposed to do?" Professor Reed said. He still did not believe there was anything to Jack's idea.

"I don't know," Jack said. "But it seems to have done something."

Robin said, "All the strange weather started right after we put the Key Stone back up. Maybe the Key Stone joined the power of Stonehenge and the power of Avebury to cause this strange weather."

"Such things cannot happen," Professor Reed said. "Your ideas go against all that science knows. Really, Robin . . ."

Just then the room went black. "The lights!" Jack shouted.

"Stay where you are, everyone," Dr. Desmond said. "I'll get a candle from Mr. Davis."

Then Robin heard the front door of the Inn open. A cold wind blew in. "What's that?" she said.

"Just the wind—" Professor Reed said.

Suddenly he cried out. The others heard him fall to the floor.

"Professor Reed!" Robin said.

Jack felt someone move past him. "Hold it!" he cried, reaching out with his one good hand. "Who are you?" He felt a strong hand push against his chest, almost knocking him down.

Jack grabbed out. His hand closed around a man's beard. But the man pulled away and ran out the door.

Leaving his beard in Jack Austin's surprised hand!

Cynthia Desmond came running back into the room with a candle. She saw Jack holding the man's black beard. Professor Reed was on the floor, trying to sit up. He was rubbing the back of his head.

"What happened?" Cynthia Desmond said.

"Someone came through the door when the lights went out," Robin said. "He hit Professor Reed on the head."

"And took the green stone," Professor Reed added, pointing to the table. "Look! It's gone!"

Jack said, "He was wearing a false beard. I grabbed it when I tried to stop him. It pulled off when he got away fron me."

Cynthia Desmond walked over and looked at the beard. She said nothing for a minute. Then she turned to Jack and Robin. "I think I know who your friend Odvard is," she said.

CHAPTER **8**

SECRET OF THE DRUIDS

All at once a flash of lightning lit up the night sky. The roar of the thunder shook the walls of the Inn. Robin looked out one of the windows. She could see someone running toward a car. "There he goes!" she cried.

They all ran out into the night. Another flash of lightning lit up the sky.

"After him!" Dr. Desmond said. "We can use the car from the Inn. I'll get the key from Mr. Davis."

"It's too late," Professor Reed said. "He is getting away."

"I don't think so," Cynthia Desmond said. "I have a pretty good idea of who he is—and where he is going."

Just then, there was a strange sound. It seemed to come from under the ground. A low, cracking noise like far-away thunder.

"What was that?" Robin said.

"I don't know," Cynthia Desmond answered. "I've never heard a sound like that before."

"Never mind," Professor Reed said. "Let's get the key and start after him."

A few minutes later, they were roaring down the dark road. Cynthia Desmond was driving. The wind was blowing the car from side to side. "I think I know where he is going," she said. "To the Key Stone. Now that he has the green stone, that is where he will go."

"Who is he?" Jack asked. "Do you know him?"

"Yes," Dr. Desmond answered. "And so do you. It's Edward Celtson."

"Who?" Professor Reed said.

"Edward Celtson. One of the men from the British Museum. The one with the black beard. He helped with the digging. You know him better by another name—Odvard."

"Of course," Robin said. "Edward Celtson. That explains everything. How he knew our names and our plans to dig. He knew because he was with the Museum."

"He wore that false beard so we wouldn't know who he really was," Jack said. "And all the while he was right next to us—working right with us."

"And trying to kill us," Robin said.

"Or maybe just trying to warn us," Cynthia Desmond put in.

"Who is he really?" Professor Reed asked Dr. Desmond.

"That I don't know," she answered. "He came to work at the Museum only a few months ago. Said he came from Wales. A very smart man. He knew a lot about Stonehenge. That's how he got the job."

"Look," Robin said, pointing up ahead. "There's the Key Stone."

They pulled off the road near the Key Stone and began walking. The wind was very strong now. Dust flew all around. Lightning flashed, but no rain fell.

Up ahead, they could see the gray shape of the Key Stone. Next to it was a man, holding something in his hands. Lightning flashed again.

It was Odvard, holding the green stone.

He turned and saw them. "Stay where you are!" he shouted. "I may be able to save us yet."

He picked up a shovel and started digging at the foot of the Key Stone.

Dr. Desmond moved forward. "Celtson!" she said. "Edward Celtson! It's me, Cynthia Desmond. We just want to talk to you!"

"There is no time to talk," Odvard answered. "I have to keep digging."

"What are you trying to do?" Jack said.

"Can't you see?" Odvard shouted. "I'm trying to move the stone."

"But you can't . . ."

Odvard was not listening. His eyes were filled with fire. He dug like a mad man.

Above the roar of the wind, there was another sound. That strange cracking, thundering sound in the ground again.

"Odvard!" Robin called. "Tell us what you are doing. Maybe we can help you."

"You have done enough already," Odvard said. "You have set off the power of Stonehenge. You didn't even know what you were doing. Even when you had the green stone."

"What is the meaning of the green stone?" Professor Reed asked. Odvard looked up and laughed.

"You—you man of science—you didn't even know that. It is in the old Druid stories. But you probably never . . ."

"Tell us what the green stone means," Dr. Desmond said.

"It is a plan," Odvard said. "A plan that tells how to control the power of the great stone circles. Together they work as a giant power lens. The lens focuses the power of the earth and sky. It can be used to make any kind of weather—snow in summer, a heat wave in winter. The Key Stone here controls it all. And the plan shows how to do it."

"But that is not—" Professor Reed said.

Odvard laughed again. "You still do not believe? Must you see all England wiped out before you do? But the Druids will not let that happen. We will save England again. Just as we did more than 3,000 years ago."

"What do you mean?" the Professor said.

"Back then, only Druids lived here. They were a happy people. They lived in peace. Their kings and queens did not believe in war. One day a man came here from across the seas. He is called the Egyptian in the old Druid stories.

"The Egyptian had a plan that he said would make the Druids even more happy. He had a plan to control the weather. That is why Stonehenge and Avebury were built. To control the weather. This green stone shows the plan with dots, circles, and lines."

"What happened?" Jack asked.

"At first, all went well. But the Egyptian was an evil man. He wanted to become the King of the Druids. Then he wanted to use the power of Stonehenge to make war on other people. He could turn their lands to ice or burn them to dust. But the Druids would not follow this evil man. So the Egyptian decided to wipe them out.

"He gave orders to move the Key Stone. The stone focuses the power of the circles. If it is moved as the plan shows, any weather can be made to happen. The Egyptian was going to kill the Druids with heat and wind because they would not make him their king.

"But the Druids tricked him. They dug under the stone. It was not tight in its hole. When the Egyptian came up to it, they pushed it on him. Then they covered the stone with dirt. They made it look like a hill so no one would ever find the evil secret under it. But you had to come here and dig. Now see what you have done."

Suddenly the ground began to shake. The cracking sound in the ground grew loud. It sounded like thunder and breaking rocks.

"Earthquake!" Robin shouted. "It's an earthquake!"

Odvard kept digging. "Help me if you want to save us!" he shouted. "We have to move the Key Stone. The power is building up. Soon it will be too late. Too strong to stop."

But the ground was now shaking so hard that no one could move without falling down.

Still, Odvard kept on working.

They saw the stone move forward about an inch.

Suddenly, a giant crack opened in the earth. It ran right up to the Key Stone. The earth shook and roared like thunder.

The crack opened around the Key Stone like a mouth. Odvard screamed and fell into the hole. The stone fell forward on top of him, breaking into two pieces as it dropped into the hole.

Then, as quickly as it had opened, the crack closed again. Odvard and the Key Stone were gone. So was the green stone.

All at once, the wind died down. The lightning and thunder stopped. The night was quiet.

"Poor Odvard," Robin said. "He tried to keep this from happening. He tried to tell us. But we wouldn't listen."

"But he did what he said he would do," Jack said. "He stopped the power of Stonehenge before it could wipe us out."

They were quiet for a minute. Then Professor Reed said, "I wonder how he knew how to read the plan on the green stone. We had tried for weeks to understand it."

Jack said, "Maybe Odvard was what he said he was—a real Druid."

"Yes," said Robin, looking at the spot where the stone had been. "And I have a feeling that he was the last of the Druids."